The Pouty Puppy

Bauer

by Denise Geremia
Illustrations by Aleesha Gosling

The Pouty Puppy

E-Book ISBN: 978-0-9918658-1-9
Paperback ISBN: 978-0-9918658-0-2

Additional copies of this book may be ordered by visiting the
PPG Online Bookstore at:

❀**PolishedPublishingGroup**
shop.polishedpublishinggroup.com

Due to the dynamic nature of the Internet, any website addresses mentioned within this book may have been changed or discontinued since publication.

For Aryn, my baby girl.
And a special dedication to Bauer,
the Pouty Puppy himself,
for making us laugh everyday,
even despite his awful life.

Dogs around town know me as
The Black Ninja.
My parents call me Bauer.
For the purpose of this story,
I will refer to myself as Bauer.
But I must make this clear:
I prefer The Black Ninja.

Once upon a time,
I was extremely loved and spoiled.
Mommy and Daddy took me for
hundreds of walks a day.

I got treats just for being cute.

I got belly rubs all day long.

Life was perfect.

Then... *she* came along.

Her... with her pink outfits, super strong hands, and sticky hugs... *she* has ruined my life.

Sometimes I pretend to like her

by eating whatever she is handing me,

but I don't like her one bit.

I wish she didn't live here.

Until I can figure out a way to get rid of her,
I will just poop as far away from Mommy and
Daddy on walks as possible.

That'll teach them.

Since *she* came along, I only get **gulp**
two, *maybe* three walks a day.
Sometimes, I only get *one*.

See how little I am loved now?

And they make me SIT for a treat!

How can anyone tell The Black Ninja to SIT?

... although Mommy does have a piece of cheese.

Ok, sit I shall, but I will not like it!

Please do not laugh at my story,
as it is not funny.
Save me. Send help.

Please.